TINY
BARBARIAN

CONQUERS
THE KRAKEN!

WRITTEN BY AME DYCKMAN ✦ ILLUSTRATED BY ASHLEY SPIRES

HARPER

An Imprint of HarperCollinsPublishers

Library of Congress Control Number: 2022947977
ISBN 978-0-06-288166-3

The artist wielded Photoshop to conquer the art in this book.
23 24 25 26 27   RTLO   10 9 8 7 6 5 4 3 2 1

First Edition

To my Barbarian Horde.
—A.D.

To Sidney, conqueror of everything!
—A.S.

This is Tiny Barbarian.

Tiny may be tiny, but he's—

MIGHTY!

With his shining helmet, his sturdy club,

and his fuzzy cape that used to be the toilet rug,

IT'S FINALLY DRY!

brave Tiny Barbarian is ready to defend his realm.

Ready to protect his family.
Ready to—

CONQUER EVERYTHING!

Just like his inspiration:

Tiny has never actually seen a Bob the Barbarian movie,
but he thinks the posters are cool.
Especially this new poster for
Bob the Barbarian Conquers the Kraken!

Just like Bob, Tiny saw himself kicking across the ocean.

He saw himself slicing through the waves.

He saw himself conquering the kraken!

There was just one problem:

I DON'T KNOW HOW TO SWIM!

(Tiny also didn't know exactly what a kraken was or where to find one.
He was taking things one step at a time.)
But as always, Tiny's mommy and daddy were there to help.
They called the Recreation Center.

And today, a very excited Tiny Barbarian embarks on his greatest adventure yet!

BYE, KITTY!
GUARD THE FORTRESS!

The quest
to conquer . . .

SWIM LESSONS! Here at the *big* community pool!

IT'S AS BIG AS THE OCEAN!

Tiny saw himself being brave.

He saw himself learning to swim.

He saw himself *not* peeing in the pool.

He just needed a few things:

First, a final potty visit.
(Even mighty Barbarians need a final potty visit.)

I FLUSHED! AND WASHED MY HANDS!

Next . . .

All this stuff!

Goggles.

COOL!

A kickboard.

AM I SUPPOSED
TO KICK IT?

ON MY HEAD?

And a swim cap to
wear on his head.

Luckily, swim caps are very stretchy.

TAKE THAT,
SWIM CAP!

But Tiny left his sturdy club and his fuzzy cape
with his mommy and daddy.
(He *knew* fuzzy capes take a really long time to dry.)

Tiny met his swim instructor,
who was very nice.

And when Tiny was ready . . .

Not yet.

Not yet.

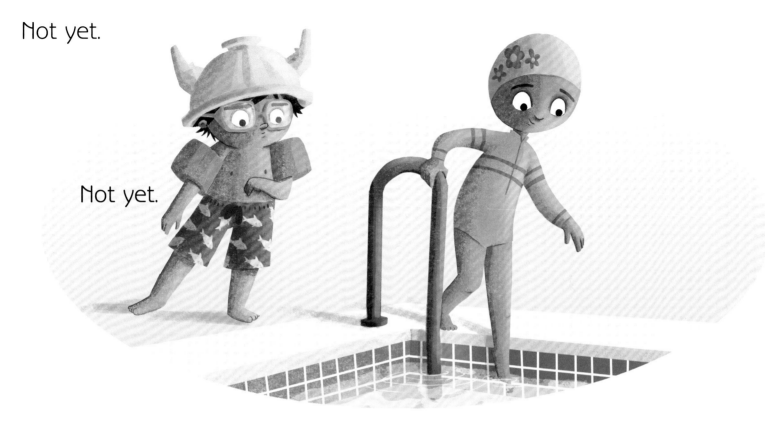

Not yet . . .

Okay!

TINY ENTERED THE POOL!

TA-DAAA!

From there . . .

Tiny learned to
hold on to the side of the pool.

He learned to
put his face in the water.

He even learned to
BLOW MIGHTY BUBBLES!

Tiny learned to float.

He learned a swimming stroke called the dog paddle.

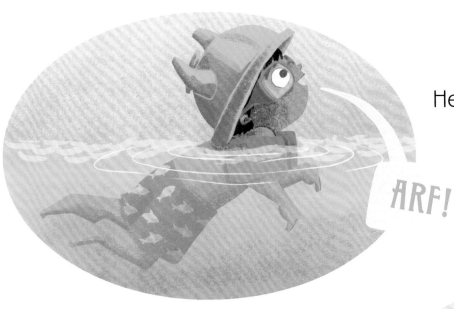

He was about to practice with his kickboard when he saw the monster.

It was a—

KRAKEN!

And it was heading straight toward
Tiny's mommy and daddy
at the far end of the pool!

Tiny had no time to run for his sturdy club!
No time to run for his fuzzy cape!
(Besides, you're not allowed to run around the pool.)

All Tiny could do was . . .

KICK!

With his new floating shield, Tiny Barbarian kicked across the ocean!

He sliced through the waves!

He rose to the challenge and issued his Battle Cry for *all* the realm to hear:

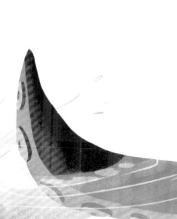

Then Tiny Barbarian

DID!

Even monsters of the deep—and the deep end—
are no match for a brave Tiny Barbarian.

His fearsome foe defeated, our triumphant hero
exited the battleground. He received:

Praise.

CLAP!
CLAP!
CLAP!

AHHH!

A dry towel.
(And dry cape.)

CONQUERED
IT!

And his First Swim
Lesson sticker.

Tiny's realm? Defended.
His family? Protected.
And he *didn't* pee in the pool.
Tiny couldn't wait to tell Kitty all about it!

But he fell asleep on the way home.
(Even mighty Barbarians fall asleep on the way home.
Especially after a big adventure.)

BUT—

Now now, Tiny. You can talk about everything—
and conquer even *more*—
tomorrow.

Sweet dreams, Tiny.